This book belongs to:

_____

_____

For my love, Ricky. Who without – there wouldn't be a book!

And Theo & Kaia, who are quite simply our world.

Riley and Ricky
Two houses, Two different homes

Copyright © 2023 Kerri Patel

Elementary font by Jes

ISBN 978-1-7384479-0-9

First paperback edition November 2023.

Nightfeed
PUBLISHING

RiLEY AND RiCKY

Two houses,
Two different homes

It was Saturday morning, on a busy, tree lined street.
Parked cars filled both sides of the road with visitors for the weekend.

Cats strolled across driveways miaowing at anyone who would feed them.

At the end of the street stood two bricked houses with large white windows, joined together by two garages.

Two houses, two very different homes.

School was out for the week and Riley woke up to the smell of bacon sandwiches her mum was making downstairs.

This was a weekend breakfast tradition for Riley and her family.

In the house next door, Ricky was also waking up late after a busy week at school, to the smell of freshly fried samosas.
Delicious triangle shaped parcels filled with vegetables and spices.

Ricky ran down the stairs and grabbed one before they reached the table.

'Serves you right for not waiting.'

'Ouch they're hot!'

'How can I when they are world famous?!' Ricky laughed.

They talked about how his Grandma had a samosa business in India, where she would make over 2000 a day!

It's been a month since Riley moved in next door to Ricky. They spent the summer holidays playing in the garden together over the fence, becoming best friends.

'What shall we play today? Catch? Tennis? I know, I know – a water fight!'

Riley can be bossy, but Ricky didn't mind, he likes playing with her.

They both giggled. Ricky, who is usually quite shy, feels comfortable around Riley.

Ricky arrived at Riley's house where she opened the door jumping with joy for her play date.

'Come in, come in.

We can play shopkeepers,

CHA-CHING!

ZOOOM!

build a rocket with magnets

or I got a brand-new karaoke machine for my birthday!'

Riley loves to sing.

'Hmm', Ricky did NOT want
to do karaoke!

'Magnets?'

'Riley, Ricky, dinner is ready!'

They ran downstairs and sat at the table which faced out to the perfectly preened garden her dad spends hours working on.

'This is my favourite dinner, shepherd's pie with broccoli on the side'.

'Yummy!'

'My mum always makes me this when I'm poorly, it makes me feel better. And I love broccoli too, they look like mini trees!' laughed Riley.

The next day, after another sunny day in the garden, Ricky asked Riley to have dinner at his house.

They sat at the table in the kitchen and Riley was wowed by the amount of different dishes that covered the table. Chicken curry, rice, salad with onions and homemade chapatis – each one perfectly round.

Ricky explained that his mum makes everything from scratch and that her curry is the best. (But everyone thinks their mum's curry is the best!)

'This looks amazing! Is it spicy?'

Ricky's mum was in the other room chatting away loudly on a video call with her friends. 'My mum could talk for England!' He said rolling his eyes.

'Mine too!' They both laughed.

Riley finished up her curry, it was like a flavour explosion in her mouth. She'd never tasted anything like it.

She was so intrigued by Ricky's culture she couldn't wait to find out more.

'Well', said Ricky hesitantly. 'My cousin is getting married next week; would you like to come? My sister Reena has something you could wear, it will fit!'

The following week, Reena picked out an outfit for Riley to wear.

'Purple and gold, my favourite colours!' She said holding it up, upside down, eager to put it on.

'Here, I'll help you', said Reena holding it up the right way round.

A silky scarf

bangles that jangle

and topped with a sparkly bindi on her forehead.

The following week, Reena picked out an outfit for Riley to wear.

'Purple and gold, my favourite colours!' She said holding it up, upside down, eager to put it on.

'Here, I'll help you', said Reena holding it up the right way round.

A silky scarf

bangles that jangle

and topped with a sparkly bindi on her forehead.

She felt like she was playing dress up, but upon arriving at the wedding she saw that everyone was wearing the same. It was the most colourful scene!

There were so many people, 200 or so, all gathered waiting to go inside. She patiently waited, but she didn't know just what she was waiting for.

Suddenly, she heard footsteps – a kind of gallop.
She looked up and the groom was arriving on a...

'WOW! Look at that!'

Riley couldn't hold her excitement. The groom, dressed in white and gold, tall with a turban on his head. The horse, white and majestic, was covered in beautiful flower garlands.

The music started, there were drums, people were dancing, waving their arms to welcome the groom.
Riley, who likes to ask questions, of course had so many!

Where does the horse live?
What happens if it needs to do a poo?
Will the horse have curry for lunch too!?

During the wedding ceremony, Riley thought it was the most magical thing she'd ever seen. There was every colour and flower you could imagine, drapes of shiny fabrics and a fire pit in the middle.

She stared in awe.

After the ceremony came dinner, more delicious Indian food. Ricky was so excited to show Riley around and they headed to the dancefloor. The music was LOUD, the dancefloor was full! People were dancing, jumping from one leg to the other, hands in the air and moving their shoulders up and down.

'It's called bhangra!' Ricky said out of breath, showing Riley how to do it. He wasn't shy on the dancefloor.

'Am I doing it right?'

'It doesn't matter, it's how you feel!'

On the way home feeling exhausted, Riley thanked Ricky for the best day EVER!

'What's next Ricky? I want to know more!'